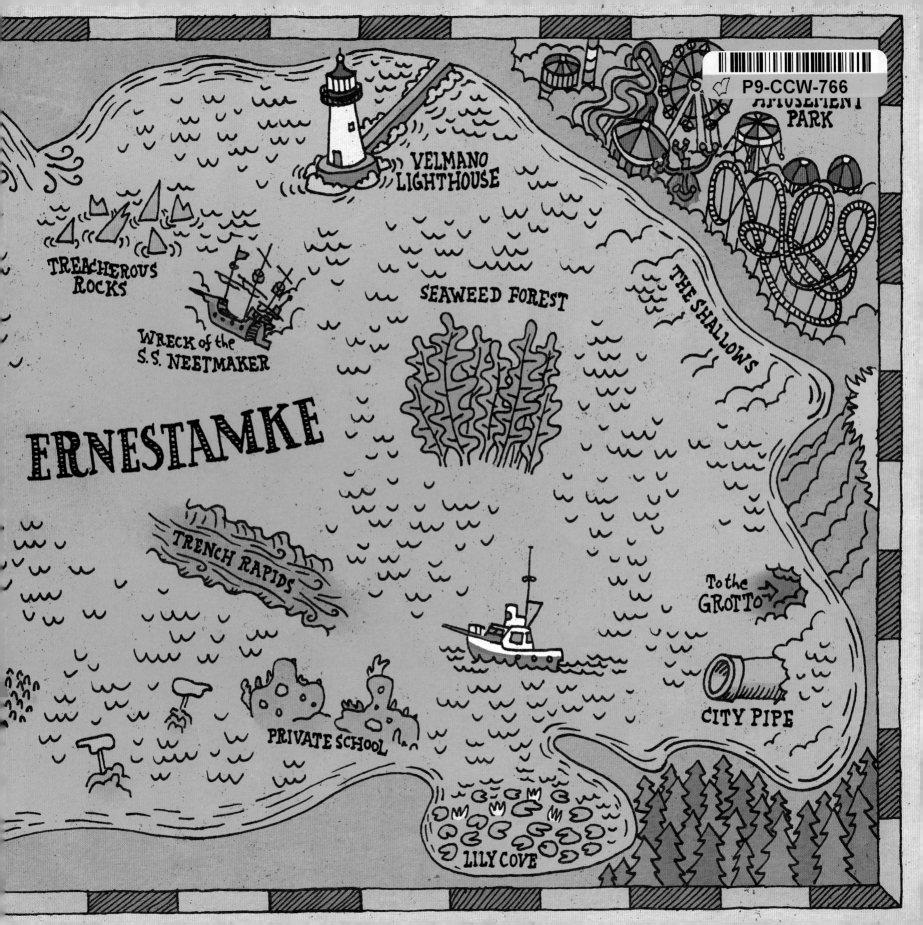

"This is it," my mother said. "You're a big sea monster now, Ernest. Remember to introduce yourself, play nicely, and use your imagination. I'm sure you'll have lots of fun."

# Sea Monster's First Day

By Kate Messner • Illustrated by Andy Rash

chronicle books san francisco

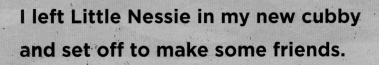

I left Little Nessie in my new cubby and set off to make some friends.

I tried joining games, but something always went wrong.

At the playground, there was no room for me on the jungle gym. And when I asked for a turn on the swings, everybody swam away.

It felt like everybody was already part of a group.

PRIVATE SCHOOL PERCH ONLY

The smallmouth bass just whispered behind my back.

He's so prehistoric.

and sang songs.

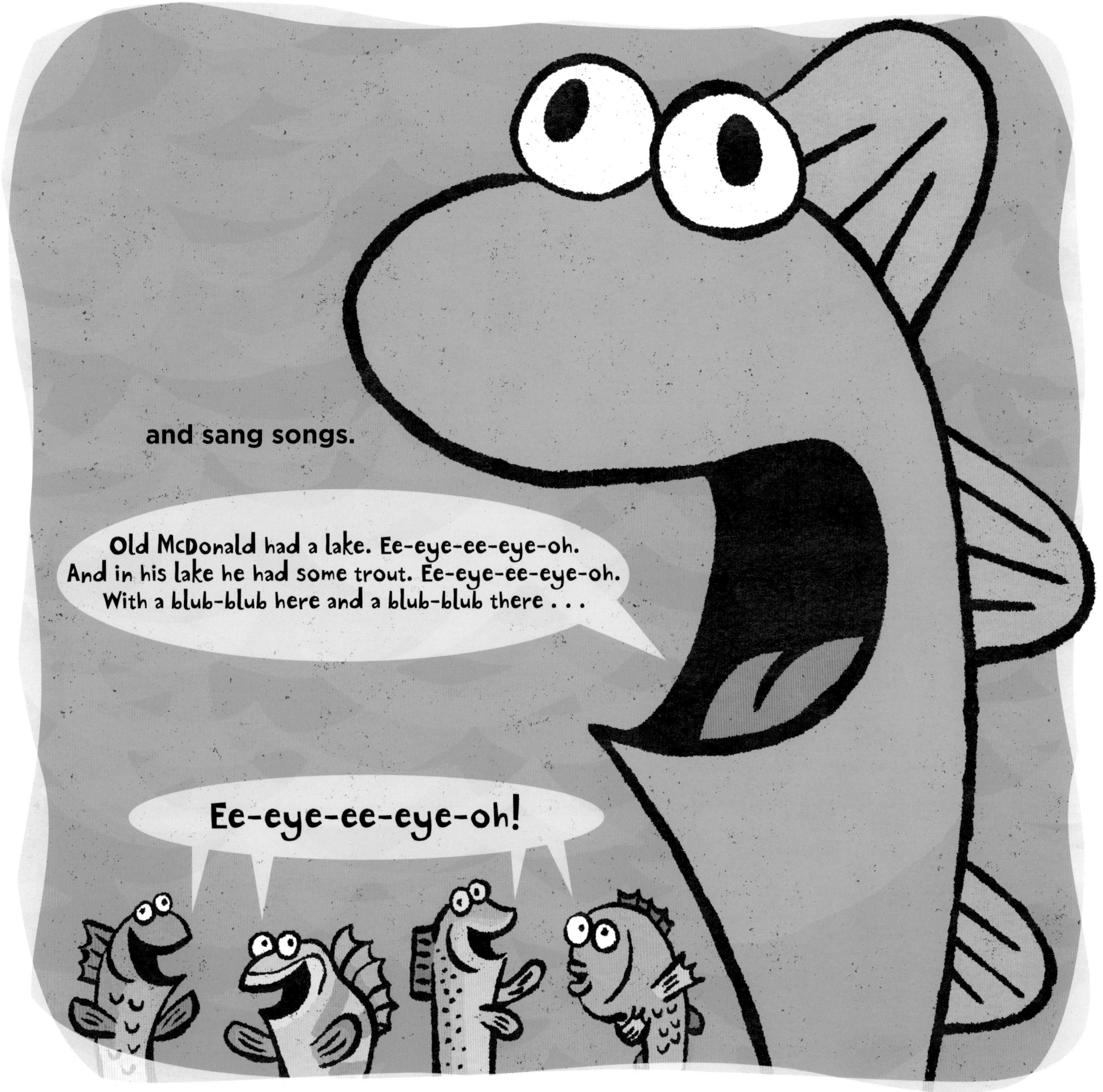

We took historical field trips . . .

and sampled tasty
aquatic plants.
Hmm . . .
a touch of algae would
go well with this.

After snack time, I played tug-of-war with the fishermen.
They kept calling me "the big one that got away."

Finally, at lunch, I spotted some fish that looked a little like me. I decided it was worth a try.

We hit it off right away. They said they were sturgeon, the biggest fish in the lake.

As we were making up games along the shore, I spotted a familiar shape, shining in the afternoon sun. A creature with strong curves, scales like mine, and a roar that shook the sky.

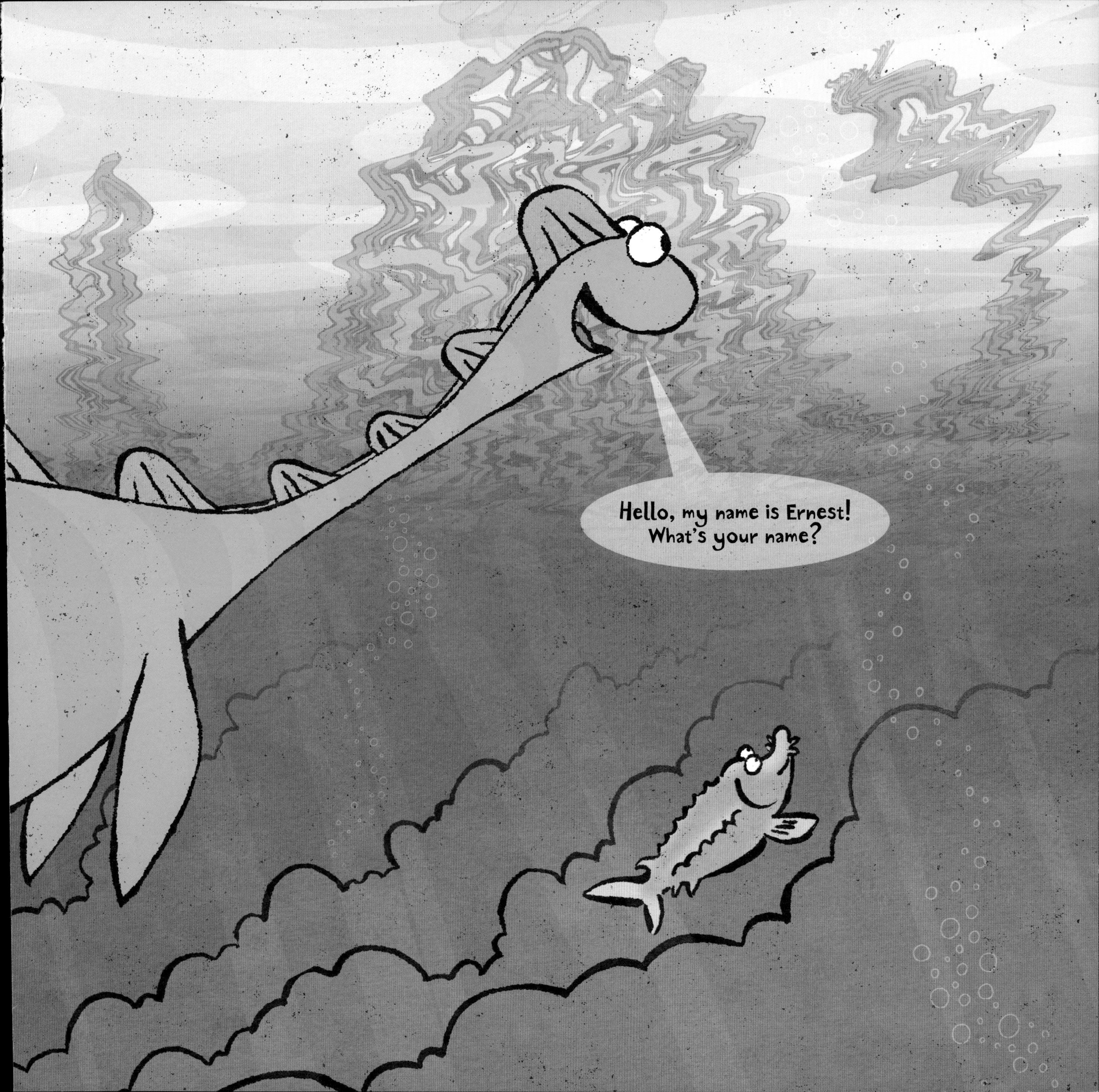
Hello, my name is Ernest! What's your name?

But that gave me an idea.

With a little imagination and my new friends, this new school was working out just fine.

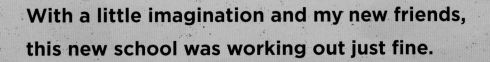

At the end of the day, Little Nessie
was right there waiting for me, and
so was Mom. I couldn't wait to tell
her about my day . . .

and my plans for tomorrow.

For Jake, who believes. —K. M.

For Joe, the new kid in
my neighborhood. —A. R.